P9-APD-439

SPIKE IN THE CITY

written and illustrated by

Paulette Bogan

PUFFIN BOOKS

PUFFIN BOOKS
Published by the Penguin Group
Penguin Putnam Books for Young Readers,
345 Hudson Street, New York, New York 10014, U.S.A.
Penguin Books Ltd, 80 Strand, London WC2R ORL, England
Penguin Books Australia Ltd, Ringwood, Victoria, Australia
Penguin Books Canada Ltd, 10 Alcorn Avenue, Toronto, Ontario, Canada M4V 3B2
Penguin Books (N.Z.) Ltd, 182-190 Wairau Road, Auckland 10, New Zealand

Penguin Books Ltd, Registered Offices: Harmondsworth, Middlesex, England

First published in the United States of America by G. P. Putnam's Sons,
a division of Penguin Putnam Books for Young Readers, 2000
Published by Puffin Books, a division of Penguin Putnam Books for Young Readers, 2002

3 5 7 9 10 8 6 4 2

Copyright © Paulette Bogan, 2000
All rights reserved

THE LIBRARY OF CONGRESS HAS CATALOGED THE G. P. PUTNAM'S SONS EDITION AS FOLLOWS:
Bogan, Paulette.
Spike in the city/ written and illustrated by Paulette Bogan. p. cm.
Summary: On Spike's first trip to the big city he rides in an elevator, catches a frisbee, and gets lost.
[1.Dogs Fiction. 2. Lost and found possessions Fiction. 3. City and town life Fiction.] I. Title.
PZ7.B6357835St 2000 [E]—dc21 99-31108 CIP
ISBN 0-399-23442-X

This edition ISBN 0-698-11809-X

Printed in the United States of America

Except in the United States of America, this book is sold subject to the condition that it shall not,
by way of trade or otherwise, be lent, re-sold, hired out, or otherwise circulated without the publisher's
prior consent in any form of binding or cover other than that in which it is published and without
a similar condition including this condition being imposed on the subsequent purchaser.

With love to

Sharon & Tony
&
My Three Angels,
Sophia, Rachael, & Lucille

Shannon was taking Spike on his first trip to the big city.

First they rode up in an elevator. "AARRROOO!" howled Spike. Someone kept stepping on his tail!

When they got to the top, Shannon let Spike go outside. He was up in the clouds with the pigeons! "YEEOWZZA!" yelped Spike. He did not feel so good.

The city streets were full of new smells.
Spike pulled hard on his leash.

"Do not get lost, Spike," Shannon said.
"Stick by me."

Spike said, "WOOF!" to his first city dog.
But the dog pretended not to hear.

At the deli, Shannon left Spike tied to a parking meter. "I will be back in a minute," she said. But Spike thought they were going to stick together.

A big truck drove by. *Splash!* Suddenly Spike was not a black-and-white dog anymore.

He was a mud-color dog! "GRRRRR," growled Spike, shaking himself off.

Spike was not sure he liked the city.

At the park Shannon let him off the leash.
Suddenly something whizzed through the air.
Spike caught it! "AARRRFFF!"

When Spike looked up, two dogs were waiting
for their frisbee. They smiled at him.
Hmmmm, thought Spike.

The dogs showed Spike a cat on a leash.
The cat did not say hello. Humpf! thought Spike.

They showed him a man on wheels.
The man was very fast.

But when a dog on a skateboard zoomed by,

Spike wanted to try it for himself. He chased it . . .

. . . under a lot of feet . . .

. . . through the middle of a million dogs . . .

. . . right by a snake with legs . . .

. . . and into a fountain full of pigeons!
"AARRGGHH!" gurgled Spike.

When Spike climbed out, the dog on the skateboard
was gone. He did not see the cat on the leash,
or the man on wheels, or his new friends.

Worse than that, Spike did not see Shannon!
"AAARROOOO!" he howled.

Spike was all alone. He did not know what to do.
He did not know how to get home. Spike sniffed
the air. He sniffed again.

He walked back around the fountain, all through
the park, and back to where he started. But this
time, no one was there . . .

. . . except Shannon! "I'm so glad I found you!"
said Shannon.

"RRRUFFF!" barked Spike. *Me too!*